THIRD-GRADE DETECTIVES #7

The Case of the Dirty Clue

by
George E. Stanley

illustrated by
Salvatore Murdocca

A L A D D I N

NEW YORK   LONDON   TORONTO   SYDNEY   SINGAPORE

To Andy and Karen and Al and Gail.
Thanks for all the Michigan memories.

First Aladdin Paperbacks edition November 2003

Text copyright © 2003 by George Edward Stanley
Illustrations copyright © 2003 by Salvatore Murdocca

ALADDIN PAPERBACKS
An imprint of Simon & Schuster Children's Publishing Division
1230 Avenue of the Americas, New York, NY 10020

Also available in a paperback edition from Aladdin Paperbacks.
Designed by Lisa Vega
The text of this book was set in 12-point Lino Letter.
Printed in the United States of America
2 4 6 8 10 9 7 5 3 1

Library of Congress Control Number 2003104291
ISBN 0-689-86358-6

Chapter One

Noelle Trocoderro gulped down her orange juice, jumped up from the breakfast table, and headed for the back door.

"Noelle!" Mrs. Trocoderro called to her. "Where are you going?"

"To Misty's house," Noelle said. "She got a new bicycle yesterday. It's stopped raining, so she wants to show it to Todd and me."

"Have you cleaned your room?" Mrs. Trocoderro asked. "You know that's your Saturday morning chore."

Noelle waved a pretend magic wand. "Ping! It's done!" she said. She gave her mother a big grin. "I got up early."

"Well, I am impressed," Mrs. Trocoderro said. "Was yesterday Misty's birthday? You didn't say anything about a party. Weren't you invited?"

"Misty didn't get the bicycle for her birthday," Noelle said. "That's not for two more months. Her aunt just sent it to her for no reason at all."

"Oh, that was nice," Mrs. Trocoderro said.

Noelle thought it was nice too, as she headed out the door.

All her friends had aunts who sent them presents even when it wasn't their birthday.

Noelle only had one uncle.

It was her mother's unmarried brother.

He hardly ever remembered to send her presents for *anything*.

Why couldn't her mother have had a sister instead?

When Noelle got to Todd's house, she picked up the morning newspaper from the sidewalk.

Noelle wished her family still took the morning newspaper.

She liked to read the comics.

Now she had to go Todd's house to do that.

Noelle's father had decided he would read newspapers on the computer to save money.

Just this morning, he told Noelle's mother about a man in Arizona who had robbed more than one hundred banks in that state.

"Pretty soon, he'll run out of Arizona banks to rob," her father said. "He'll have to go somewhere else."

"Mr. Merlin must have read that same story, Dad," Noelle told her father. "That's exactly what he said."

Mr. Merlin was Noelle's third-grade teacher.

His class was known as the Third-Grade Detectives.

They helped the police solve crimes.

Sometimes, Mr. Merlin's friend, Dr. Smiley, helped them.

She had a police laboratory in the basement of her home.

All of the girls in Mr. Merlin's class wanted to be like Dr. Smiley.

So did a lot of the boys.

"Why are you and Mr. Merlin interested in what people in Arizona do, Dad?" Noelle asked. "It's a long way from where we live."

"The world is getting smaller every day,

Noelle," her father said. "If it can happen in Arizona, it can happen here."

That's funny, Noelle thought. *Mr. Merlin is always saying things like that too.*

Todd opened the front door before Noelle could ring the bell. "I'm ready to go," he said.

Noelle handed him the newspaper. "Don't throw this away until I find out what happened to Bennie and his dog."

"Okay," Todd said. He took the newspaper and laid it on a table by the door.

When Noelle and Todd got to the corner of Misty's block, they stopped.

"Look, Todd!" Noelle said. "Why is Misty standing in the middle of the street?"

Noelle and Todd ran up to her.

Misty was crying.

"What's wrong?" Noelle asked.

Misty pointed to something that used to look like a bicycle.

"Oh!" Noelle said. "You had an accident!"

"No, I didn't! My little brother, Paulie, left it in the middle of the street," Misty said. "A car ran over it. Now it's all bent. And it's covered with red dirt, too. It used to be so pretty and clean."

Noelle swiped off some of the red dirt with her finger. "Yuck!" she said.

"What are you going to do for a bicycle to ride?" Todd asked.

Misty shrugged and wiped away a tear. "Will you help me carry it into the garage?" she asked.

Noelle, Todd, and Misty picked up Misty's bent bicycle.

They took it to her garage and laid it in a corner.

"I want to find the person who did this," Misty said. "He or she is going to buy me a new bicycle!"

A mystery! Noelle thought.

"I think this is a case for the Third-Grade Detectives!" she said.

Chapter Two

Just then, Mrs. Goforth came out to the garage.

Paulie was hiding behind her.

"Let's see how bad it is, Misty," Mrs. Goforth said.

Misty sniffed and showed her mother the bicycle.

"Oh, goodness!" Mrs. Goforth said. "I don't think anyone can fix that."

"Of course not," Misty sobbed. "It's ruined."

She gave Paulie a dirty look.

"I'm sorry," Paulie said.

"You should be," Misty said.

She looked around the garage.

She spotted a old blanket.

She spread it over her bicycle.

"I don't want anything else to happen to it," she said.

Noelle looked at Todd.

She couldn't imagine what else could happen to the bicycle.

"When I feel better, I'm going to give it a bath," Misty said.

"I want to wash off that ugly red dirt.

"After that, I'm going to show it to the police.

"They'll find out who did this.

"I have a description of the car!"

"You do?" Noelle said. "That's very important evidence!"

"Well, I can see you have another case to solve," Mrs. Goforth said.

Noelle, Todd, and Misty nodded.

"We need to write down everything that happened," Noelle said. "You should always do that while it's still fresh in your mind."

"That's what Mr. Merlin says," Todd agreed.

Noelle and Todd followed Misty to the den.

Misty got a yellow pencil and a big red tablet.

She gave them to Noelle.

Then they all plopped down on the floor in front of the television set.

"Okay," Misty began.

"My aunt sent me this beautiful bicycle.

"It's the prettiest one in town.

"I don't think anybody else . . ."

Noelle held up her hand. "The police won't be interested in that, Misty," she said.

"They only want to know about the crime," Todd added.

Misty took a deep breath. "Okay. Well, Paulie went out to the garage and got on my bicycle.

"He rode it down the driveway and into the street.

"The street was still slick from the rain.

"Paulie fell over and skinned his knee.

"He left the bicycle where it was and came running into the house.

"He told us what happened.

"Mother said for me to get the bicycle out of the street.

"I was on the front porch when I saw this white car come by.

"It was going really fast.

"It drove right over my bicycle.

"I screamed, 'Mother! A car just ran over my bicycle!'

"Then I rushed out to see how bad it was.

"That's when you and Todd came running up.

"You know everything else."

Noelle thought for a minute. "There's one problem, Misty. This may not be a crime," she said. "It might just be an *accident*."

Misty gave her a puzzled look.

"I think the police will say that your bicycle shouldn't have been in the middle of the street in the first place," Noelle explained.

Misty looked like she was going to cry again.

"Wait a minute, Noelle!" Todd said. "I think it *is* a crime!"

"Why?" Noelle asked.

"The white car was speeding," Todd said. "That's against the law."

"Todd's right, Noelle!" Misty said. "If it hadn't been going so fast, it wouldn't have run over my bicycle."

11

"You two have forgotten something very important," Noelle said. "The police have to *see* a car speeding before it's illegal."

Misty let out a big sigh.

"Don't worry, Misty. We can still look for the white car," Todd said. "Let's start calling the rest of the Third-Grade Detectives right now."

Chapter Three

Misty telephoned Leon Dennis and Amber Lee Johnson and told them what had happened.

Amber Lee wanted to know the make, the model, and the year of the white car.

Misty put her hand over the mouth of the receiver.

She told Noelle and Todd what Amber Lee was asking.

"I don't know what she means," Misty said.

"I do," Noelle said. "My father is always looking for cars on the computer.

"The *make* means the *brand*—like Chevrolet, Chrysler, or Ford.

"The *model* means the *style*—like Impala, Stratus, or Explorer.

"The *year* means when it was made."

"Except that cars usually come out the year before," Todd added.

"This is getting too hard for me," Misty said. "The only thing I know about the car is that it was white."

"Misty, I need to talk to Amber Lee," Noelle said. "Put the telephone on speaker."

Misty pushed a button.

"Amber Lee, this is Noelle," Noelle said.

"For the time being, just look for *white* cars.

"And keep a record of the ones you see."

"What are we going to do with all this information when we get it?" Amber Lee asked.

"We'll give it to the police," Noelle said.

"Then maybe we can have a lineup of suspect *cars*—just like the police do with suspect *people*," Misty said.

"I'll look at each car and pick out the one that ran over my bicycle."

"That sounds more like a parade to me, Misty. And it would take forever," Amber Lee said. "Besides, whoever heard of a *car* lineup?"

Noelle knew that Amber Lee was just jealous because she wasn't in charge.

"Well, we may get lucky, Amber Lee. Misty might also recognize the car while we're walking around town," Noelle said. "Do you have a better idea?"

"No," Amber Lee said.

But Noelle knew that Amber Lee wouldn't stop trying to think of one.

So she decided she needed to give Amber Lee a job.

"Will you call the rest of the Third-Grade Detectives?" Noelle asked.

Amber Lee let out a big sigh. "Okay," she said. "I'll tell them to start looking for white cars too."

"Good. In two hours, we'll meet you downtown at JoAnn's family's restaurant," Noelle said. "We'll compare our lists."

Just as Misty, Noelle, and Todd started to leave the den, Mrs. Goforth said, "Detectives need energy! There are brownies and cold milk on the kitchen table!"

"Yes!" Todd said.

"Thank you, Mrs. Goforth," Noelle said.

They decided to have three brownies each to make sure they didn't get hungry while they were looking for white cars.

When they left Misty's house, Misty said, "Where do you think we should start?"

"I think we just need to start walking," Noelle told them.

"When we see a white car, Todd and I will give you the information and you can write it down in your red tablet."

They walked around Misty's block.

They didn't see any white cars.

They walked over to Noelle's house.

They saw one white car.

"I don't think that was the car that ran over my bicycle," Misty said, "but I'm not sure."

"You still need to write down the information about it—just in case the police let us have a lineup," Noelle said.

She told Misty the make and the model.

Todd said he thought it was a brand-new car.

Misty added that.

The three of them circled the block and headed to Todd's house.

Three white cars whizzed by.

"Did you get the information?" Misty said.

"Only for the last one," Todd said.

He gave Misty the make, the model, and the year.

"I don't agree, Todd," Noelle said. "You got the make and the year right, but you got the model wrong."

Misty marked out what Todd had said and wrote down what Noelle told her.

"Well, they look alike," Todd complained.

After they had walked around another block, Noelle said, "We need to go downtown.

"It's time to meet the rest of the Third-Grade Detectives.

"Maybe we'll see some more white cars on the way."

Noelle was right.

Five white cars passed them.

But Noelle and Todd were able to give Misty descriptions of only three of them.

"This isn't working," Misty said.

"I don't know the *make,* the *model,* or the *year* of the car that ran over my bicycle!

"It could be one of the cars we miss!"

Noelle and Todd agreed.

"When we get to JoAnn's restaurant, we need to think up a better way to solve this mystery," Noelle said.

Chapter Four

When Noelle, Todd, and Misty got to JoAnn's restaurant, JoAnn, Amber Lee, and Leon were sitting at a back table.

"Nobody else could come," Amber Lee told them, "but they all said they'd look for white cars for the lineup."

"Well, we're not sure a lineup is going to work," Todd said.

"We looked for white cars on the way to the restaurant," Noelle added.

"But some of them were driving too fast."

"I bet one of them was the car that ran over my bicycle," Misty said. "It was also driving too fast!"

"I'm sorry your bicycle got run over, Misty," Leon said.

"Me, too. It was so pretty and clean when it

came yesterday," Misty said. "Now it's all bent and covered with red dirt."

"I've never seen *red* dirt before," Leon said. "Where did that come from?"

Misty shrugged.

"Did you see any white cars?" Noelle asked them.

"A few," JoAnn said. "But they were also going too fast."

"I'm sure I'd recognize the car if I saw it again," Misty said, "but I can't describe it to you."

"That's too bad," Amber Lee said. "It doesn't leave us much to go on."

"No, it doesn't," Noelle agreed.

"I think we're going to have to ask Mr. Merlin for a secret code clue," Todd said.

Mr. Merlin used to be a spy.

He knew lots of secret codes.

When the Third-Grade Detectives had trouble solving a mystery, Mr. Merlin gave them a secret code clue to help.

He told them that working with secret codes was good for their brains. And all the Third-Grade Detectives wanted to have good brains.

"Do you think we should still look for white cars until Monday?" Misty said. "I just know I'd recognize it if I saw it."

Since the Third-Grade Detectives couldn't think of anything else to do, they all said, "Yes."

After they ate the snacks that JoAnn's father fixed for them, they walked around town and looked for white cars.

They found several parked along the street.

But Misty still didn't recognize any of them.

Finally, Noelle and Todd walked with Misty back to her house.

They didn't see any more white cars along the way.

"I have an idea," Noelle said.

"What?" Todd asked.

"Instead of walking around, we can sit on Misty's front porch all day tomorrow and see if that white car drives by again," Noelle said. "It's called a *stakeout*. The police do it all the time."

"That's a really great idea," Todd said. "If the white car drove by one time, it might drive by another time."

"I think it sounds really boring," Misty said.

"Misty, sometimes police work is boring," Noelle said, "but it has to be done in order to solve the crime."

"Oh, all right," Misty agreed reluctantly.

Early the next morning, Noelle and Todd met Misty on her front porch.

They played games.

They read books.

They even did some of their schoolwork.

But they didn't see any white cars.

By noon, they were really bored.

But Mrs. Goforth made them a picnic lunch.

Later, she brought them some snacks.

"I hope I never have to go on a *stakeout* again," Misty said.

Right before Noelle and Todd went home, a white car drove slowly down the street.

It belonged to Mrs. Robinson, one of the second-grade teachers.

"Is that it?" Noelle cried. "Is Mrs. Robinson returning to the scene of the crime?"

Misty ran out to the street to get a look at the back of the car.

"No, that's not it!" she cried. "Mrs. Robinson didn't run over my bicycle."

The next morning at school, Noelle told Mr. Merlin they had a new mystery.

Misty gave him the details.

Mr. Merlin picked up a piece of chalk. "Here's a secret code clue," he said. "It should put you on the right track."

On the board he wrote:

BKKS GKN RCNP

Chapter Five

Noelle quickly wrote down on a sheet of paper the secret code.

First, she tested it with secret codes that Mr. Merlin had used before.

But it wasn't one where the message starts at *X* and goes around in a circle like the hands of a clock.

And it also wasn't a number code, a reverse alphabet code, or a shift code, either.

Noelle sighed. "I was hoping it might be an old code," she whispered to Todd. "It isn't."

"Mr. Merlin has never given us the same secret code twice," Todd said.

"There's always a first time," Noelle said.

"Hey! Look at Misty," Todd said. "Why isn't she working on the secret code?"

Noelle looked.

Misty was walking around the room.

She was whispering something to everyone.

When she got to Noelle's desk, she whispered, "My aunt is giving a fifty-dollar reward to whoever solves the mystery."

"Fifty dollars!" Noelle exclaimed.

"That's a fortune!" Todd said.

"I know! But my aunt is really mad that someone ran over my bicycle," Misty said.

"It's my job to find out who solves the mystery *first*.

"I'm supposed to call her right away."

"Well, excuse us, Misty," Noelle said, "but we really need to get back to work."

"You'd better hurry," Misty said. "Amber Lee thinks she's almost there."

But fifteen minutes later, no one had solved the secret code clue.

Mr. Merlin told them to put away their papers and to get out their math books.

Noelle was disappointed.

She really wanted to win that reward.

In her mind she had already started a list of things she would buy with the fifty dollars.

During lunch, the only thing the Third-Grade Detectives talked about was the fifty-dollar reward.

"You don't get the money if you don't solve the mystery," Misty reminded them.

When they all got back to class, Noelle said, "Mr. Merlin! We need some help!"

If the Third-Grade Detectives had trouble solving a code, Mr. Merlin sometimes gave them a hint.

"All right. The key to this code is what you are," Mr. Merlin said. "And I'll let you work on it for fifteen more minutes, but that will be all today."

Noelle and Todd huddled together across the aisle.

"What are we?" Noelle asked. "Girls, boys, kids, students, *what*?"

"I know! We're the *Third-Grade Detectives*!" Todd said. "That must be what Mr. Merlin means. But what's the secret code?"

"Mr. Merlin said that the key to the code is

what we are," Noelle said, "so if Third-Grade Detectives is the key, then . . ." She stopped. "Todd!" she whispered. "I think I know!"

Mr. Merlin had a big, thick code book on his desk.

If you finished your work early, he let you look through it.

Noelle and Todd did that a lot.

"I remember a *key word* code," Noelle said. "That's what it's called, even though sometimes there's more than one word."

She wrote down THIRD-GRADE DETEC-TIVES.

She marked through all of the duplicate letters.

That left THIRDGAECVS.

She followed THIRDGAECVS with the remaining letters of the alphabet:

T H I R D G A E C V S B F J K L M N O P Q U W X Y Z

Below that, she wrote the regular alphabet:

A B C D E F G H I J K L M N O P Q R S T U V W X Y Z

Then Noelle decoded the secret code clue.

She found a letter in the key word code alphabet and looked below it in the regular alphabet:

BKKS GKN RCNP became LOOK FOR DIRT.

Noelle raised her hand.

She told the class what the secret code clue was.

"I almost solved it too, Mr. Merlin," Amber Lee said.

Noelle looked at Todd and rolled her eyes.

"She always says that," Todd whispered.

"But what does it *mean*?" Misty asked.

"That's what the Third-Grade Detectives have to figure out," Mr. Merlin said.

Everyone groaned.

Todd looked at Noelle.

Noelle nodded her head.

She was sure she knew *exactly* what "Look for dirt" meant.

Chapter Six

When school was over, everyone hurried outside.

"I don't understand the secret code," Misty said. "Why does Mr. Merlin want us to look for dirt?"

"Mr. Merlin doesn't want us to look for dirt, Misty," Noelle said.

"He doesn't?" Misty said.

"No," Noelle said. She grinned. "I think he wants us to look for *dirty white cars*!"

"Hey!" Leon shouted. "There goes one now!"

Sure enough, a dirty white car was pulling out of the school parking lot.

Misty shook her head. "That's not it," she said.

"I don't think it's a very good clue," Amber Lee said.

"Yes, it is," Noelle said. "Now we'll only have to look for *dirty* white cars this afternoon."

"That's what police do, Amber Lee," Todd said. "They narrow down the suspects."

Amber Lee stamped her foot. "Well, I can't go with you. I have my piano lesson!" she said. "You'll probably find the dirty white car and solve the mystery without me. You'll win the fifty-dollar reward."

"I can't go either. I have gymnastics," Leon said. "I'm going to make it to the Olympics."

"I have to fold napkins at the restaurant," JoAnn said. "But I can help you after that."

"Then here's what we'll do," Noelle said. "Misty, Todd, and I will look for dirty white cars and make a list of the ones we find.

"We'll meet you at JoAnn's restaurant after you've finished with your lessons.

"Together, we'll take the list to the Police Department."

Everyone except Amber Lee agreed that would work.

"You'll still get the fifty-dollar reward for solving the mystery," she said.

But when Noelle, Todd, and Misty got to JoAnn's restaurant, they had nothing to report.

Noelle was disappointed.

Her list of things to buy with the fifty dollars kept getting longer.

"Everybody must have gone to the car wash this weekend," Noelle said.

"The only dirty white car we saw was the one at school."

"We're stumped," Todd said. He looked at Amber Lee. "You were right. It's not a very good clue."

"Maybe Mr. Merlin meant look for dirt some-place else," Misty suggested.

The Third-Grade Detectives thought about that for a minute.

Finally, Noelle said, "I don't think so. I'm sure it has something to do with finding a dirty car."

The next morning, Mr. Merlin said they were going to study science because it would help them solve Misty's mystery.

That caused a lot of excitement among the Third-Grade Detectives.

"Let's talk about dirt," Mr. Merlin said.

Todd and Noelle looked at each other.

"*Dirt* was part of the secret code clue!" Noelle whispered.

"Right!" Todd agreed. "We really need to pay attention to this."

"Dirt is also called *soil*," Mr. Merlin continued.

"Soil is different in different parts of the country.

"Soil can be ash-gray, black, brown, brown-orange, gray-brown, red, or yellow.

"The color of the soil depends on what kinds of minerals are in it.

"Most of the soil in our part of the country is either ash-gray or gray-brown."

Noelle thought about that.

She didn't think those were very pretty colors. They were too *dirty*.

Noelle wished they had red or yellow soil.

She liked those colors.

"For tomorrow, I want you to bring some soil to class," Mr. Merlin said. "We'll study it and see what we can find."

All during spelling and reading, Noelle kept trying to think of where her relatives lived.

Did they have red or yellow soil there? she wondered.

If they did, would they send her a sample of it overnight—like some of her father's business mail?

Noelle really wanted to go to school the next day with some dirt that didn't look *dirty*!

At recess, Misty said, "I'm glad I didn't wash my bicycle after all!"

"Why not?" Noelle asked.

"It still has that red dirt all over it," Misty said. "That's what I'm going to bring!"

Chapter Seven

Noelle moped all the way to school.

Todd had a small glass bottle of yellow dirt.

"Mom and Dad got this on their honey-moon," he said. "It's from Yellowstone National Park."

"You're so lucky," Noelle said.

She had a jar of ugly-looking gray dirt from her mother's flower garden.

Everywhere she looked in her neighborhood, the dirt was the same color.

Boring! Boring! Boring! Noelle thought.

In class, Mr. Merlin had the students line up their jars on a long table.

Several people had brought "special" dirt that their families had gotten on vacation.

Noelle couldn't believe her parents had never thought about doing that.

She was so disappointed.

Didn't it occur to them that their daughter might need some pretty dirt in class one day?

Well, Noelle knew one thing for sure.

She was never ever going on a vacation again without bringing back jars of dirt from everywhere they went.

Noelle didn't care if it took ten jars.

Or a hundred!

Or even a thousand!

Mr. Merlin taped a big map of the United States on the wall.

It showed what kind of dirt was found in all of the states.

Some states were mostly yellow.

Some states were mostly black.

Some states were mostly red.

Some states were made up of several colors.

Noelle's state was mostly gray.

One by one, Mr. Merlin told the class about the soil samples.

He showed them on the map where the dirt had come from.

When he got to Misty's red dirt, he said, "Where did you go to get this?"

"My garage," Misty replied.

Mr. Merlin blinked. "I don't understand," he said.

"That red dirt was on my bicycle after the car ran over it," Misty explained.

"I scraped it off and put it in that little jar."

Mr. Merlin smiled. "Good work, Misty! I was hoping someone would think to *look for dirt* on your bicycle," he said. "Now I need to do a test on it."

Noelle looked over at Todd.

"He didn't do tests on the other dirt," she whispered. "Why is Misty's dirt so important?"

Todd shrugged.

"This may take several minutes," Mr. Merlin said.

"Get out your spelling books and study all of the words that start with *Z*.

"We'll have a test on them tomorrow."

Noelle didn't want to study words that started with Z.

She wanted to watch Mr. Merlin test Misty's red dirt.

She was sure it had something to do with solving the mystery of who had run over Misty's bicycle.

But she got out her spelling book, anyway.

Silently, she spelled *z-e-b-r-a, z-e-r-o, z-i-p-p-e-r,* and *z-o-o.*

Then she peeked over her spelling book to watch Mr. Merlin.

He got out a microscope.

He put some of Misty's red dirt on a glass slide.

He looked at it under the microscope.

Then Mr. Merlin walked over to his bookcase and took a big book off the shelf.

He read several pages.

Then he looked through the microscope again.

"That's strange," he said.

"What's strange?" Leon asked.

"This red dirt is found only in Arizona," Mr. Merlin told the class.

He walked to the map.

He pointed to Arizona.

"It's a long way from here," he said.

"What does that mean?" Amber Lee asked.

"Dirt collects on the bottoms of cars," Mr. Merlin said.

"It stays there until something knocks it off.

"In this case, the dirt shook off when the car ran over Misty's bicycle.

"I would say that car had recently been in Arizona."

Noelle quickly raised her hand. "I think we should look for a dirty white car that has Arizona license plates!"

"That's a very good suggestion, Noelle," Mr. Merlin said. "You might just solve the mystery if you find one!"

Noelle hoped so.

Her list of things to buy with the fifty-dollar reward was now three pages long.

Chapter Eight

After school, several of the Third-Grade Detectives met on the playground.

"This is just like a real police case!" Noelle said.

"We keep getting closer and closer to the criminal.

"First, we only had a white car.

"Then we had a *dirty* white car.

"And now we have a dirty white car *with an Arizona license plate*."

"Well, I think we would have been closer sooner, Noelle, but you got us all confused," Amber Lee said.

"That secret code clue didn't say *look for dirty cars*.

"It said *look for dirt*.

"All this time we should have been looking *under* the cars!"

Noelle knew that Amber Lee was *technically* right.

When most people thought of *dirty* cars, they thought of what you could see.

They didn't think about the *bottoms* of cars.

But if the bottom of a car had dirt on it, it was still *dirty*.

Suddenly, Noelle knew what to say. "Amber Lee, a good detective looks *everywhere* for evidence.

"I planned to look *underneath* all these white cars too!

"If the bottom of a car is dirty, then it's still a *dirty car*!"

"Well, I think we should look for *any* white car that has an Arizona license plate," Amber Lee said. "The person who ran over Misty's bicycle might have washed the car since then."

Everyone agreed that Amber Lee was right.

Sometimes Amber Lee made Noelle so mad.

Amber Lee thought she was the best detective in the class.

It had been her idea to start the Dr. Smiley Fan Club.

And Amber Lee was still the president.

That meant Amber Lee felt she was in charge of every case the Third-Grade Detectives worked on.

Wrong! Noelle thought.

But Mr. Merlin didn't like for the Third-Grade Detectives to argue.

He said that wasn't very *professional.*

He told them they should always work together.

Noelle took a deep breath.

Finally, she said, "Amber Lee has a good point. We'll look for both clean and dirty cars with Arizona license plates!"

"What if the driver was just visiting in Arizona?" Leon asked. "What if he doesn't live there?"

"Leon has a good point too," Todd said.

"Okay," Noelle said. "Here's what we'll do."

She couldn't believe how complicated detective work was.

"We'll look for *clean and dirty* white cars *with*

46

and without Arizona license plates," she said.

"I think we're back where we started," Leon said.

"Well, I think we're wasting time just talking about it," Noelle said.

"Right!" Todd said. "We need to *do* something."

They decided to divide up the town.

They thought that would make it easier.

"At dinnertime, we can meet at our restaurant," JoAnn said. "My father will cook hamburgers for us."

"That's a great idea," Noelle said.

The Third-Grade Detectives all headed off in different directions.

"I still think we need to look for a dirty white car with an Arizona license plate," Noelle said.

"I don't know, Noelle. Maybe Leon was right," Todd said. "Whoever was driving the car might have only been visiting in Arizona."

"On television, detectives talk about *instinct*, Todd," Noelle said.

"That means sometimes they just *feel* they're right about a case.

"This is one of those times.

"It takes a while for dirt to build up underneath a car.

"I think that car had been in Arizona for more than just a short visit."

From the school, Noelle and Todd walked downtown to the courthouse square.

They saw several white cars parked in front of stores.

Some of them were dirty.

Noelle checked out the license plates.

Most were from their state, but some were from Michigan and Oklahoma.

There were none from Arizona.

So Noelle decided not to look underneath any of them.

Finally, it was time to meet at JoAnn's restaurant.

Everyone else was waiting for them.

When they were all seated at a table in the back of the restaurant, Todd said, "Did anybody find a dirty white car with an Arizona license plate?"

No one had.

Noelle sighed. "The dirty white car could have left town," she said. "It may have gone back home to Arizona."

Chapter Nine

The next morning, Noelle said, "I think the dirty white car has gone back to Arizona, Mr. Merlin."

"Well, Noelle, it certainly could have. But you don't know that for sure," Mr. Merlin said.

"And a good detective never assumes anything.

"He or she investigates every possibility before coming to a final conclusion.

"So I'm going to give you one more secret code clue to help you do that."

Usually, that made the Third-Grade Detectives happy.

But this time they didn't say anything.

Most of them believed Noelle was right.

The dirty white car had probably left town.

Noelle thought Mr. Merlin looked disappointed.

Amber Lee stood up. "As president of the Dr. Smiley Fan Club, I say we don't give up!"

The class applauded.

Noelle stood up too. "I wasn't going to give up, Mr. Merlin."

Anyway, Noelle thought, she couldn't give up.

Her list of things to buy with the fifty-dollar reward was now up to five pages!

"Well, I honestly didn't think any of you would, class," Mr. Merlin said.

He walked to the chalkboard.

He wrote:

DJJC AH SOGR VNM DJQO

"I'll even tell you that it's another key word code," he said.

"And the *key word* is something I'm always telling you and what I'm proud that you remembered.

"Now, I'll let you work on it in groups for fifteen minutes."

Noelle, Todd, and Misty pulled their desks together.

"This is really hard," Misty whispered. "What is Mr. Merlin always telling us that we remembered?"

"Open your spelling books."

"Now, it's time to study science."

"We'll work on the secret code clue tomorrow."

"Straighten your desks."

"Have a good weekend."

"Well yes, he says all of those things," Todd agreed, "but I think the *key word* is something we've just been talking about."

Noelle grinned. "*Never* give up!" she said.

"Right!" Todd said. "Let's test it and see!"

He wrote out NEVER GIVE UP.

He crossed out the duplicate letters: NEVRGIUP.

He wrote out the key word alphabet.

Underneath it, he wrote out the regular alphabet:

N E V R G I U P A B C D F H J K L M O Q S T W X Y Z

A B C D E F G H I J K L M N O P Q R S T U V W X Y Z

🚲 🚲 🚲 🚲

Noelle studied the secret code clue: DJJC AH SOGR VNM DJQO

D in the key word alphabet was *L* in the regular alphabet. She decoded the rest of the message: LOOK IN USED CAR LOTS.

"Yes!" Noelle cried. "That's the one place we haven't looked for the white car!"

Noelle told Mr. Merlin what the secret code clue was.

"Why do we have to look there?" Amber Lee asked.

"I'll tell you after you've done your detective work," Mr. Merlin said.

There were five used-car lots in town.

So after school, the Third-Grade Detectives broke up into two groups.

Noelle and Todd would search two of the lots.

The rest of the Detectives would search the remaining three. "When we finish, we'll meet at JoAnn's restaurant," Noelle said. "We'll compare notes."

"We can also have snacks," JoAnn offered.

First, Noelle and Todd headed for Billy Bower's Best Buys.

When they got there, Noelle told Billy that they were looking for a dirty white car with Arizona license plates.

"I've got plenty of dirty white cars," Billy told them, "but I don't have one with Arizona license plates."

Noelle started to leave, but Todd said, "Maybe we should look underneath them just in case."

"Do you mind?" Noelle asked Billy.

Billy shrugged. "Be my guest," he said.

"If we don't find a white car with an Arizona license plate," Todd said, "we may have to start looking underneath all the other white cars in town."

Noelle hoped not.

That sounded like really dirty work.

But she also knew that police officers sometimes had to start their investigations all over.

For the next several minutes, Noelle and Todd looked underneath all of Billy Bower's white cars.

"No red dirt anywhere," Noelle said. "It's all this ugly gray color."

Next, Noelle and Todd headed for Carl's Car Barn.

When Noelle told Carl what they were looking for, Carl said, "Well, young lady, you're in luck!

"It's parked at the back of the lot.

"I'd show it to you myself, but I have another customer."

Noelle and Todd hurried to the back of the lot.

They found the white car.

It wasn't dirty.

But it had Arizona license plates.

Noelle and Todd got down on their knees and looked underneath the car.

"Red dirt!" Todd said excitedly. "I think we may have solved this mystery!"

"I think so too," Noelle said.

She took an envelope out of her pocket.

She scraped off some of the red dirt into it.

"But first we need to test it in Dr. Smiley's laboratory," she added. "We'll use Carl's phone to call JoAnn's restaurant and tell the rest of the Third-Grade Detectives to meet us there instead."

Chapter Ten

"We're in luck!" Noelle said as they turned the corner of Dr. Smiley's block.

"That's Dr. Smiley's car coming down the street!"

Noelle and Todd waited for Dr. Smiley on her front porch.

"We think we've solved the mystery!" Noelle called to her.

"But first we need to test some dirt in your laboratory," Todd added.

"Great! Mr. Merlin has been telling me about your new case," Dr. Smiley said. "If you two will grab a bag of groceries, we'll get started faster."

Noelle and Todd each got one of the brown bags.

Noelle could tell that hers had ice cream and cookies in it.

Just thinking about that made her hungry.

Dr. Smiley always had snacks for them when they came to her house.

After they put away the food, Noelle handed Dr. Smiley the envelope with the red dirt.

"I'll go set up the lab equipment," Dr. Smiley said. "I'll also call Mr. Merlin and tell him to bring over the soil sample from Misty's bicycle."

The rest of the Third-Grade Detectives and Mr. Merlin arrived a few minutes later.

Dr. Smiley said, "First, I'm going to test this sample of red soil that Noelle and Todd got from the bottom of the white car.

"If it matches what Misty brought to class, I think we've found the car that ran over her bicycle."

Dr. Smiley put some of Noelle and Todd's dirt on a slide.

She looked at it under her microscope.

She wrote something down on a piece of paper.

Then Dr. Merlin handed Misty's dirt to her.

She put some of it on a slide and looked at it under another microscope.

When she finished, she took another look at the first slide.

"Well, it's the same, all right," she said. "The soil on Misty's bicycle came from underneath the car at Carl's Car Barn.

"A car tends to build up layers of soil under the fenders and the body.

"But the rain that day had softened it.

"So when the car hit Misty's bicycle, some of the soil fell off.

"When you find the suspect car, you can compare the soil left at the scene of the crime—Misty's bicycle—with the soil underneath the car.

"This can help prove that the car was there."

"What do we do now?" Noelle asked.

"I need to call my aunt," Misty said. "I have to tell her to send Noelle and Todd the fifty-dollar reward."

Amber Lee started pouting, but she didn't say anything.

"I need to talk to Carl," Dr. Smiley said. "He

should have the name of the person he bought the car from."

While the Third-Grade Detectives ate cookies and ice cream, Dr. Smiley talked to Carl. After that, she made another call to the Police Department.

The Third-Grade Detectives were eating their second helping when Dr. Smiley's doorbell rang.

Dr. Smiley answered it.

A police officer came inside.

"We want to thank the Third-Grade Detectives!" she said.

The Third-Grade Detectives looked at one another.

Noelle knew they had solved the mystery of who had run over Misty's bicycle. But why would the police thank them for that?

"We found the man who sold the white car," the police officer continued.

"He's from Arizona.

"He robbed a lot of banks there.

"Now he's going around to other states.

"He was just about to leave to rob one of our banks.

"If it hadn't been for the Third-Grade Detectives, we might not have caught him!"

"Oh, wow! Mr. Merlin and my dad read about him on the computer several days ago!" Noelle said. "I should have paid more attention."

Mr. Merlin grinned. "When I realized that Misty's red dirt was from Arizona, I wondered if the person who ran over her bicycle might also be the bank robber."

"And that's not all," the police officer continued. "There's a big reward for his capture!"

The Third-Grade Detectives cheered.

Noelle knew she had to say something.

She had decided to do it when her list of things to buy reached ten pages.

"I think we should give all the reward money to our school—including the fifty dollars from Misty's aunt," Noelle said.

The rest of the Third-Grade Detectives agreed.

"Why did the man from Arizona sell his car?" Noelle asked Mr. Merlin.

"That happens a lot," Mr. Merlin said.

"A criminal comes to a town to commit a crime.

"But he does something—like run over a bicycle—that might cause people to notice his car.

"The criminal realizes he has to get rid of that car, so he trades it in for another one.

"The police are still looking for someone driving the *first* car.

"By the time they discover that the criminal has traded in the first car, it's too late.

"The criminal has committed the crime and gone on to another town."

Noelle looked over at Todd. "Dirt tells a lot of stories!"

"Is everyone still hungry?" Dr. Smiley asked.

"Yes!" the Third-Grade Detectives cried.

"Well, we're going to have chocolate ice cream, crushed cookies, and gummy worms!" Dr. Smiley said.

"What's that called?" Noelle asked.

"A *dirt* sundae!" Dr. Smiley said.

Trace That Car!

Have an adult (a parent or a teacher) call a large, privately owned used-car lot in your town (for several reasons, it's important that it not be a used-car lot associated with a national dealership, because the automobiles there are often thoroughly cleaned) and ask the owner if you can collect soil samples from underneath the fenders and bottoms of cars with out-of-state license plates—the farther away from your state, the better. Be sure to tell the owner that you're doing a forensic (police) science experiment. You might also have to explain to him or her that it's normal for soil to build up underneath cars and that you're not accusing him or her of selling dirty cars!!

At the used-car lot, scrape off soil samples

from automobiles from various states. Try to get soil that has collected next to the metal, as this will usually give you the most accurate information.

In a geology book (that a parent or a teacher can get for you), find a soil map of the United States and compare the samples of soil you obtained to it.

If a used car has a Texas license place, for instance, do you think the soil you found actually came from Texas?

If there are several types (colors) of soil in Texas, then which part of the state did your soil come from?

If you don't believe the soil you found actually came from Texas, then where do you think it came from?

Hint: Think about how the car from Texas got to your state. Sometimes these cars are put onto big trucks and then driven to other states to be sold. Sometimes, though, used-car dealers hire people to drive used cars from state to state. If the car from Texas was *driven* from Texas to your state, what other states did it go through? Do you think the soil came from one of those states?

These are all things that forensic (police) scientists have to think about.

Remember what Noelle said in *The Case of the Dirty Clue*: "Dirt tells a lot of stories." What stories does your dirt tell?

What's next for the Third-Grade Detectives?
Here's a sneak preview of their next case,

The Secret of the Wooden Witness.

Chapter One

Todd Sloan was in the kitchen.

His grandmother had told him he could fix a peanut butter and jelly sandwich for a snack.

But Todd couldn't decide which kind of jelly he wanted: grape, plum, or red raspberry.

Just then his grandmother shouted, "Todd! Come quick! You need to see this!"

Todd raced into the living room.

His grandmother was sitting in front of the television.

She always stayed with him until his parents got home from work.

Todd saw Dr. Smiley's face on the screen.

Dr. Smiley was a friend of his teacher's, Mr. Merlin.

She was also a very important police officer.

Todd's class was known as the Third-Grade Detectives.

Sometimes Dr. Smiley helped them solve local mysteries.

"Dr. Smiley is moving to another town," his grandmother said.

Todd stared at her. "She can't do that!" he said.

He looked back at the television screen.

Now they were showing pictures of a PTA talent show.

Todd didn't want to see little kids dancing. He wanted to hear more about Dr. Smiley.

"I'm sorry, Todd," his grandmother said. "They'll probably have more information about her on the later news."

Todd couldn't wait for that.

He had to find out right away what was happening.

He went back to the kitchen.

He dialed Noelle Trocoderro's number.

Noelle was his best friend in Mr. Merlin's class.

When Noelle answered, Todd said, "Dr. Smiley is leaving! She's moving to another town."

Noelle gasped. "How do you know that?" she asked.

"I saw her on television," Todd said.

"This is bad for the Third-Grade Detectives, Noelle!

"I think we need to have an emergency meeting right now."

"I can't, Todd," Noelle said.

"I have to go with my mother to Greene's Department Store.

"Do you want to come with us?"

Todd didn't really like shopping with Noelle and her mother.

It was so boring.

But he had to talk to Noelle about Dr. Smiley.

They had to figure out what to do.

"I'm sure my grandmother will say yes," Todd said.

"Good!" Noelle said. "We'll be by your house in ten minutes."

Todd told his grandmother that Noelle and her mother had invited him to go to Greene's Department Store with them.

His grandmother said it was okay.

Todd was standing on the front porch when Mrs. Trocoderro pulled into his driveway.

He climbed into the backseat with Noelle.

For several minutes they whispered about Dr. Smiley.

Finally Noelle said, "Mom? Why would Dr. Smiley move to another town?"

"She probably got a better job," Mrs. Trocoderro said.

"How could it be *better*?" Noelle asked.

"She has a laboratory in the basement of her house.

"She has a fan club.

"She has the Third-Grade Detectives to help her solve crimes."

"The new job might pay more money," Mrs. Trocoderro said.

"But what will Mr. Merlin do?" Todd asked. "I

always thought he and Dr. Smiley were a couple."

Mrs. Trocoderro shrugged. "Well, maybe Mr. Merlin will be leaving too," she said.

"Oh, no!" Noelle said.

"What will happen to the Third-Grade Detectives if *both* Mr. Merlin and Dr. Smiley leave?" Todd said.

THIRD-GRADE DETECTIVES

Everyone in the third grade loves the new teacher, Mr. Merlin.
Mr. Merlin used to be a spy, and he knows all about secret codes and the strange and gross ways the police solve mysteries.

YOU CAN HELP DECODE THE CLUES AND SOLVE THE MYSTERY IN THESE OTHER STORIES ABOUT THE THIRD-GRADE DETECTIVES:

- #1 The Clue of the Left-handed Envelope
- #2 The Puzzle of the Pretty Pink Handkerchief
- #3 The Mystery of the Hairy Tomatoes
- #4 The Cobweb Confession
- #5 The Riddle of the Stolen Sand
- #6 The Secret of the Green Skin
- #7 The Case of the Dirty Clue

Coming Soon: #8 The Secret of the Wooden Witness

ADDIN PAPERBACKS • Simon & Schuster Children's Publishing • www.SimonSaysKids.com